MW00800079

A Shirt Full of Skunks!

Little Stinker Series
Book 2

Dave Sargent was born and raised on a dairy farm in northwest Arkansas. When he began writing in 1990, he made a decision to dedicate the remainder of his life to encouraging children to read and write. He is very good with students and teachers alike. He and his wife Pat travel across the United States together. They write about animals with character traits. They are good at showing how animals act a lot like kids.

A Shirt Full of Skunks

Little Stinker Series
Book 2

By Dave Sargent

Illustrated by Elaine Woodward

Ozark Publishing, Inc.
P.O. Box 228
Prairie Grove, AR 72753

Cataloging-in-Publication Data

Sargent, Dave, 1941–
    A shirt full of skunks / by Dave Sargent ;
illustrated by Elaine Woodward. —Prairie
Grove, AR : Ozark Publishing, c2007.
    p. cm. (Little stinker series ; 2)

    "Be honest"—Cover.
    SUMMARY: When Dave finds a den of
baby skunks, he stuffs them in his shirt and
takes them home with him. He must find a
safe place to hide them.
    ISBN 1-59381-276-0 (hc)
            1-59381-277-9 (pbk)

    1. Skunks—Juvenile fiction.
2. Dogs—Juvenile fiction.
[1. Games—Fiction.]
I. Woodward, Elaine, 1956– ill.
II. Title. III. Series.

    PZ7.S243Sh 2007
    [Fic]—dc21   2005906108

Inspired by

my pet skunk Sammy.

Dedicated to

all animal lovers.

Foreword

When Dave finds a den of baby skunks, he stuffs them inside his shirt and takes them home with him. He finds a place to hide them. That night at the supper table, his brother and sister tell their mama that her beans stink! Mama discovers that the smell is on Dave! She sends him outside!

Contents

If you'd like to have Dave Sargent, the author of the Little Stinker Series, visit your school free of charge, call: 1-800-321-5671.

One

A Shirt Full of Skunks!

I heard Mom yelling at the top of her lungs, "Dave! Dave! You'd better get home right now! It's way past chore time!"

I yelled, "Coming, Mama."

I sure hated to leave those little skunks. They were so cute. One of them was solid white. It had pink eyes and a pink nose. It was the cutest one of all. But I knew that if my mama knew I had them, she wouldn't let me keep them.

I started to leave but I stopped
and looked down. I couldn't leave
those little skunks behind. I gathered
them all up and stuffed them inside
my shirt. They were crawling around
and they tickled me.

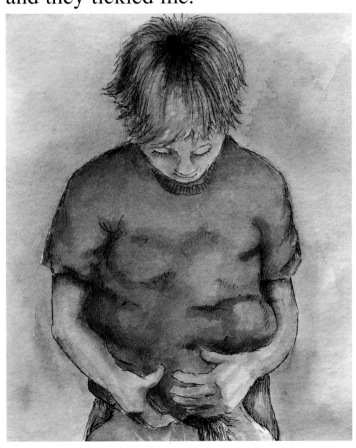

Just as I walked out of the woods, I saw Mama in the front yard. I slipped around behind the house and then eased in the back door and up the stairs. I looked for a place to hide the little skunks. There was no safe place to hide them.

Sitting on the chest of drawers was an old shoe box that I kept all of my valuables in. It was full of all kinds of things. I collected marbles, funny-looking rocks, bottle caps and little pieces of colored glass. I put all my valuables in one of the drawers.

I punched some holes in the lid with a pencil. I put the little skunks in the shoe box. Then I put the lid on it and slid it under my bed.

Two

These Beans Stink!

I ran to the chicken house and fed the chickens. Then I gathered the eggs and took them to the house. I got the slop, took it to the corn crib, mixed some shorts in it and fed it to the hogs.

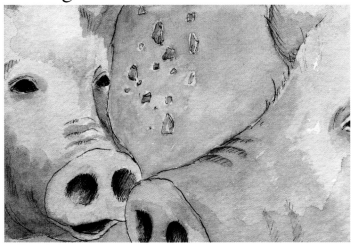

All I had left to do was feed the baby calves some warm milk. Dad was finishing up the milking. I got enough milk to feed the baby calves and they ate fast. Boy, I had rushed through my chores today to keep from getting into trouble.

After all the chores were done and everyone was back in the house, we scrubbed up for supper. Mom was a great cook and tonight she had made my favorite foods. We were having pinto beans and fried taters plus meatloaf, cornbread and gravy.

We took our places at the table. I had three brothers and one sister. One brother and one sister were twins. They were fifteen months younger than I.

They fought all the time so I had to sit between them at the table. Emily and Emery, the twins, had started dishing out the beans when Emily wrinkled her nose and said, "Mom, these beans stink!"

Then Emery drew in a deep breath and added, "They really do, Mom! They smell bad!"

Three

Banned from the Table

Mom knew the beans couldn't smell bad. She was the best cook in the whole wide world! Where she was sitting, she couldn't smell a thing. Dad shrugged his shoulders. He couldn't smell anything either.

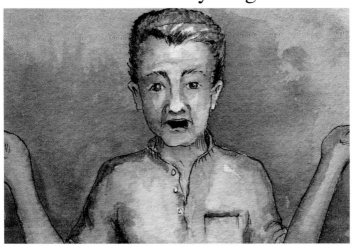

Mom and Dad told Emily and Emery that they must be imagining things. The twins tried to eat but couldn't. Since I couldn't smell, it didn't bother me. I was pigging out on my favorite foods.

Mom got up and walked slowly around the table, sniffing the air. When she got around by Emily, she said, "I do smell something now."

When she got close to me, she said, "Phewee! I smell a skunk!"

She looked down at me and demanded, "Dave, what in tarnation have you been doing?"

"Nothing, Mama," I replied.

"Nothing my eye! You've either been sprayed by a skunk or you've been playing with one!" she yelled.

"I promise, Mama. I haven't been doing anything," I said.

Mom looked at me and asked, "Do you really think I'm a fool?"

"No, Mama," I replied.

"Take your plate outside and eat!" she ordered.

"Yes, Mama," I said. I picked up my plate and walked out.

Four

Skunk Facts

Skunks have strong front legs and sharp claws. These claws are good for digging a den.

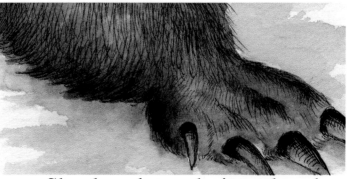

Skunks sleep during the day. They hunt at night, walking along, catching insects and looking for fruit. They sniff out field mice, squirrels, gophers, moles and chipmunks.